The Christmas Candle

The Christmas Candle

BY RICHARD PAUL EVANS

PAINTINGS BY JACOB COLLINS

Simon & Schuster Books for Young Readers

I would like to acknowledge the following people: Laurie Liss for her continual faith and friendship. Jacob Collins for his extraordinary paintings—it is an honor to share these pages with him. Ann Brashares for her sensitivity and love in the handling of this story. Rick Richter and Stephanie Owens Lurie and the rest of the Simon & Schuster Children's Publishing Division. Laurie Chittenden for additional editing assistance. Those with whom I have the pleasure to serve on The Christmas Box House International, Inc.™ board, especially my mother and father, David and June Evans, Jim Anderson and Judy Schiffman, whose efforts affect the lives of innumerable children, Jenna, Allyson, Abigail, McKenna, and Michael.

And always, Keri.

SIMON & SCHUSTER BOOKS FOR YOUNG READERS
An imprint of Simon & Schuster Children's Publishing Division
1230 Avenue of the Americas, New York, New York 10020

Book design by Edward Miller
The text of this book is set in 16-pt. Weiss.
The illustrations are rendered in oil paint.
Printed in the United States of America

10 9 8 7 6 5 4

Library of Congress Cataloging-in-Publication Data

Evans, Richard Paul.
The Christmas candle / by Richard Paul Evans :
illustrated by Jacob Collins. — 1st ed.
p.   cm.
Summary: On Christmas Eve, Thomas buys a magical candle that changes the way he
views his fellow human beings and helps him feel charity for those less fortunate than he.
ISBN 0-689-82319-3
[1. Christmas—Fiction. 2. Generosity—Fiction. 3. Magic—Fiction.]
I. Collins, Jacob, ill. II. Title.
PZ7.E89227Ch   1998   [Fic]—dc21   98-4392
CIP   AC

Produced by 17th Street Productions,
a division of Daniel Weiss Associates, Inc.
33 West 17th Street, New York, NY 10011

*O*n a snowy Christmas Eve a young man made his way along a dark, deserted cobblestone street. His name was Thomas, and he was wrapped in a woolen cloak, a knapsack flung across his back. In his hand hung a tin candle lantern. Behind the lantern's glass panes sat the remains of a spent candle.

When he saw the glow of candlelight through the shop window of the chandler, the village candle maker, he hurried his steps, turning onto the snow-covered pathway. In Thomas's way stood a beggar, shaking his cup for coins. Thomas pushed him aside impatiently and opened the door to the shop.

Inside the shop, metal pots filled with tallow and beeswax hung from a stone hearth. The old chandler stood with his sculptor's tools in his hands, surrounded by the beautiful creations he had made out of wax.

"I am lucky to find you here," Thomas said. "The town is empty."

The old man gazed silently at Thomas as the young man glanced about at the rows of sculpted candles. There were sprites and fairies, angels with see-through wings, and fragile princesses in gowns as delicate as lace. They smelled of myrrh and frankincense and meadow flowers.

"You are a foolish old man," Thomas said. "You spend hours making beautiful things that devour themselves. How long before the flame melts an angel into an ugly clump of wax?" He pointed to a row of simpler candles. "I only need light. I will take one of those."

The chandler looked steadily at Thomas. "The Christmas candles are of no good to you."

Thomas was startled by the stern response, but he laughed. "It would do me much good not to stumble in the dark. Are you playing me, old man? I will not pay more for your candle than it is worth."

"It is only four coppers . . . but you may find it costly." The old man's words were strangely serious.

"I have money! Give me the candle!" Thomas shouted. "It is late, and my family is waiting for me. I need illumination to find my way."

"Then it is *illumination* you desire?" the chandler asked softly.

"That is what I need," Thomas replied.

The candle maker nodded slowly. "So you do." He took a candle, dipped it over a flame, then placed it inside the lantern's tin frame.

Thomas dropped some coins on the counter and walked to the door.

The old man's lips pursed in an odd, amused smile. "Merry Christmas, my brother," he said.

The farewell surprised Thomas. "To you, as well," he stammered. Then he hastily stepped out into the darkness, the lantern lighting the road ahead.

Thomas had traveled only a short distance when a shadow emerged from an alleyway. *A robber,* he thought fearfully. He held out his lantern. "Who's there?" he called. Then, in the light of the candle, he saw it was only a frail woman huddled against the cold.

"Sir," cried the woman. "A pence, please?"

His eyes narrowed in contempt at the beggar. Then, as he looked at her more closely, he gasped. He knew the face well! It was his own mother!

"Mother! What is this prank? Why do you greet me as a beggar!"

The woman stared at him. "Just a ha' pence, Sir?"

"Why are you here? Where are my brothers? My sister?" Thomas asked. He reached out to her, but she pulled away. "Mother, how peculiar you act. You will catch a chill. Here, take my cloak." He removed it and held it out to her.

Cautiously, the woman came forward, then snatched the coat and retreated into the shadows.

But as she moved from the lantern's light, her appearance changed. She was not his mother, but a beggar indeed! With Thomas's cloak in hand, she disappeared into the darkness.

"A strange trick," he said to himself. He wrapped his arms around his chest, wishing he had kept his cloak. "It is I who will catch a chill."

Thomas walked on, quickening his pace against the frigid air. As he passed beneath the awning of a darkened inn, the candle revealed another form, lying in the gutter. He held out the candle and again gasped. "Has the universe gone mad? Elin, my brother! Are you sick?"

He set the lantern down, and pulled his brother's limp arm around his shoulder, struggling to lift him. "Elin, I cannot carry you."

He pounded on the inn's door, which was opened by a grim-faced woman.

"My brother is sick and I fear he will freeze before I can come back for him. May I bring him inside?"

"For the price of a night," she cackled. "A shilling."

"A shilling?" Thomas reached into his pocket. "I have only sixpence."

The old woman scowled and began to shut the door.

"Wait! My knapsack is worth more than a shilling!" Thomas cried. "And the trousers inside are newly tailored. I will give you everything."

The old innkeeper looked at the bundle, then reached out a fat hand.

Thomas flung his knapsack from his back and handed it to her with the last of his money. She opened the door. "Bring him in."

Leaving the lantern on the curb, Thomas dragged the man into the inn's foyer. As he gently laid him on the wooden floor he suddenly saw that the man's face, like the beggar's, had changed.

"So it is your brother who lay in my gutter?" croaked the woman.

Thomas gaped at the man. "He . . . he is not my brother. . . ."

"You are mad," the woman muttered, and she shoved him out the door.

Outside, Thomas picked up his lantern.

He looked into its glass panes. "There is something strange about your light," he whispered.

Thomas had just glimpsed the bright lights of home when he came across a little girl shivering in the cold.

"Have you anything to eat, Sir?" she asked in a faint voice.

Thomas felt a stir in his chest. This child was tiny, no bigger than his sister. . . . Suddenly he pulled the lantern away. He wouldn't shine it in her face. He could guess its trick. And what could he do for this poor waif? He had no food or money left to give.

"I have nothing," Thomas murmured as he left her, willing himself not to turn around.

Penniless and cold, Thomas trudged onward, hardly glancing at the familiar houses of his childhood.

His own home was dressed for the season, and music and laughter came from inside. As he entered the foyer, his mother greeted him with great excitement. "Thomas," she exclaimed, "you have arrived!"

Hearing her cry, his sister and brothers rushed into the room to welcome his arrival.

When the joviality had begun to settle his mother looked at him peculiarly. "Thomas, where is your cloak?"

"Yes," said his brother Elin, "and why have you no pack?"

Thomas gazed solemnly into their bewildered faces. "I . . . gave everything away," he said.

"To whom?" his mother asked, puzzled.

Thomas looked down at the waning Christmas candle. "The old man spoke the truth. You are costly . . ." A smile of understanding slowly spread across his face.

". . . but of great worth."

"What is this riddle? What old man?" his sister asked.

"A wise man who sculpts candles," Thomas replied as he gazed at the face of his sister. And just then, in his mind, her bright face became the woeful, hungry face of the poor child in the cold.

Thomas looked at the sumptuous banquet laid out on the table. Suddenly he turned to the door.

"Thomas, where are you going?" his sister asked.

"I must see about another member of our family," he said.

And as he left the warm, fragrant house for the cold night, Thomas's heart was warm with joy. For that Christmas Eve, a lesson was learned and taken to heart: If we will see things as they truly are, we will find that all, from great to small, belong to one family. And this truth, known from the beginning of time, is perhaps seen best in the joyous illumination of Christmas.

"What is the most important thing we can do for our children?"

In 1996, The Christmas Box Foundation sponsored a children's welfare conference to discuss this question. Their answer: *The Christmas Box House International, Inc.*™—a "one-stop" shelter in Salt Lake City, Utah, for children waiting to be placed in foster homes. Currently, abused and neglected children are bounced between various agencies—police, doctors, lawyers, and case-workers—before being thrust into a new home. At The Christmas Box House, these visits all occur on-site, providing familiarity and comfort at a difficult time. The child's first sight upon entering the home is an enormous Christmas tree with his or her very own toy underneath. To help fund this haven for neglected children, all of the author's proceeds from this book will go toward the construction of The Christmas Box House. If you are interested in buying a brick, or would like more information, write to:

P.O. Box 1416
Salt Lake City, Utah 84110

www.thechristmasbox.com

Richard Paul Evans is the best-selling author of *The Christmas Box*, *Timepiece*, *The Letter*, and *The Locket*. He is also the founder and executive director of The Christmas Box Foundation and The Christmas Box House International, Inc.,™ a nonprofit organization devoted to the building of shelter-assessment facilities for abused children. Mr. Evans has donated all of his proceeds from this book to The Christmas Box House.

He lives in Salt Lake City, Utah, with his wife, Keri, and their five children. He is currently working on his next children's book and his next novel.

A leading American Realist, **Jacob Collins**'s work has been featured in one-man and group shows throughout the world. Mr. Collins is the founder of the Water Street Atelier in Brooklyn, New York, where he teaches drawing and painting. *The Christmas Candle* is his first book. He lives in Brooklyn with his wife and son.